For Liam
I hope that my words Touch you

[signature]

HER
VISION
QUEST

A MEMORY CALLING

TIM HALEY

 **FriesenPress**

Suite 300 - 990 Fort St
Victoria, BC, Canada, V8V 3K2
www.friesenpress.com

ISBN
978-1-4602-5079-2 (Hardcover)
978-1-4602-5080-8 (Paperback)
978-1-4602-5081-5 (eBook)

1. Juvenile Fiction, Action & Adventure

Distributed to the trade by The Ingram Book Company

CONTENTS

This Book is Dedicated
To All My Children

ACKNOWLEDGMENTS:

Sekai Haley.

My partner and best friend who has given me the space to write this book and the patience to understand cultural differences.

Shirley Dickie.

Her first name was the inspiration for me to use as our heroine's name and the first to read the rough draft with inspiring feedback.

Wedlidi Speck.

First Nations Hereditary Chief of the Gixsan Clan of Fort Rupert who helped me to understand the significance of the "Vision Quest" as perceived by The North American First Nation's People.

HER
VISION
QUEST

INTRODUCTION

Though the Vision Quest is associated with North American Native traditions, it has been practiced all over the world by other cultures past and present. In Scandinavia and Northern Europe, the term Out-Sitting is used to describe the same spiritual search. In this practice, a young person just before puberty goes into the wilderness in search of their calling. Many times this exercise is accompanied with fasting and in some cultures, a hallucinogenic herb is ingested. He or she is usually accompanied by a Spirit Guardian Animal, which will help the young person along their way. In the west coast native custom, it is usually a boy who heads out to find his spiritual direction, but it has occurred occasionally that a young girl will be called upon to do so. The coming into adulthood and the understanding of life's direction is the motivation behind this practice. This story is an enactment of this spiritual pursuit filled with high adventure, mysticism and magic.

CHAPTER 1

"Time to get up," Shirley's father quietly urged through her partially opened door. "Be sure to put on warm under clothes. It's minus ten outside."

Shirley groggily sat up, uncovering herself from her warm blankets. Stepping on the cold floor helped her to get dressed quickly. When she entered the kitchen, her father was holding a cup of coffee and offered her hot chocolate from his other hand.

After strapping on their backpacks and grabbing the rifles, father and daughter braved the outside chill. The sun had not yet risen but its glow hung over the mountain they were about to climb.

"Where do you think the best place would be for us to go?" asked her dad.

"Well, the breeze is coming from the north so we should head up the gully and then turn south along the ridge," boasted Shirley, glad that her father took pride in her knowledge of the mountains.

They walked silently for the better part of three hours, both steeped in their own thoughts. There had been no sign of deer as the animals were being elusive. The sun had risen over the mountains, casting a shaft of light that reached over Shirley and her father, illuminating the hills beyond.

It began to warm and the snow at Shirley's feet started to soften, exposing the ice underneath. The morning was now full in their faces when suddenly she heard a crack and then a groan. She glanced over to where her father had been. Out of the corner of her eye she saw him sliding down an embankment.

"Dad!" she screamed.

Frightened, Shirley ran back to where she saw her father fall and looked over the ledge. He was wedged up against a tree and just beyond was a gaping ravine.

"Are you all right?" she yelled.

There was no response.

"What do I do?" She asked herself. "Think, Shirley. I can't go down there. It's too slippery!" Then it dawned on her. "There's a rope in my pack that we brought to string up the deer carcass."

She fumbled through the bag until it was in her hands. Tying one end of the rope with a bowline knot to a tree, she flung the other over the ledge down to her father. Grabbing the rope, she inched her way down the slope to where he lay. He was still breathing.

"Dad, can you hear me?" she muttered in a shaky voice.

There was no answer. Shirley removed her coat and spread it over her father.

"The coat and sun will keep him warm until I can bring help," she thought, "but home is three hours away."

She remembered then that on the other side of the slope was a cabin that their neighbors used as a hunting retreat. She stashed her rifle and pack in a thicket to make her load lighter and headed up the incline. She found a deer trail, which made the going easier.

Shirley reached the top in record time and looked down through the trees, seeing smoke rising from the cabin.

Running hard, she yelled, "Is anyone there?"

Opening the door and peering in, she took a quick look around. "Hello? Hello?" she implored. The cabin was empty.

Shirley ran to the back, finding the neighbor's hobbled horse grazing on scattered hay.

"A horse," she thought. She remembered seeing a hackamore bridle hanging on the wall and a sack of horse meal in the corner.

Shirley flew back into the cabin, grabbing the halter and a handful of oats. The horse jerked his head up with ears pushed forward and steam billowing out of his nostrils as she approached with an outstretched hand, cooing as she slowly walked toward him. In a moment, her arms were around his neck, slipping the bridle over his warm snout.

Shirley struggled back up the slope and down the other side, pulling hard at the begrudging horse, taking half an hour to get back to her father's side. This time her dad was conscious and responding to his daughter.

"I can't move my leg," he groaned.

"I can't haul you up by myself. Can you hold onto the rope if I wrap it around you?" she asked.

"Yes," he answered. "I'll try."

Shirley tied the rope around his waist and gave it to him to hold. She struggled back toward the horse. Out of the corner of her eye and through the stand of trees high up toward the top of the mountain, she spotted what seemed to be an opening to a cave. She did not pay too much attention at the time as she was determined to get her father up to the trail.

Reaching the horse, she put the other end of the rope around his neck and pulled on the bridle. Slowly, her father was brought up to the trail. He was able to get on the back of the horse using his good leg and Shirley as a boost.

It took three grueling hours for them to reach home. Shirley's big sister was chopping wood outside and saw them as they approached.

"What happened?" Molly cried.

Just then, the girls' mother came out.

"Dad is hurt," yelled Shirley.

"Quick, help me get your father into the van. We'll take him to town," said her mother. "We may have to take him as far as the Comox hospital later."

The road to town was bumpy and Shirley could hear her father groan as the van lurched each time. It was not long though before a doctor from the clinic was looking into the back of the vehicle, listening to Shirley's account. He said her father needed to be airlifted to the hospital in Comox. He rushed in to make the necessary arrangements.

"Molly, you and Shirley drive back home and I will go with your father to the hospital," her mother announced. "I will phone you from there to let you know how things are going."

Sitting at home waiting for the phone call, Shirley could not get her mind off the events earlier that day. After a few hours of sitting and fidgeting, the phone range.

"Your father is going to be okay," her mother said from the other end. "Are you okay, Shirley?"

"Yes, now I am," Shirley said with relief in her voice. "I'll let Molly know."

"I'll be here in Comox for a couple of days until your father can ride in a car to come home. Our friends here will be able to give us a lift back."

"Okay. Thank you, Mom. Bye." Shirley put down the phone and rushed outside to tell Molly the news.

Coming back inside, Shirley flopped down in the couch and began to shake violently from overtaxed emotions and sheer exhaustion. Molly came in and saw her sister's state.

Concerned, Molly asked, "Are you alright?"

"I'll be fine," Shirley faltered.

After a quarter of an hour, Shirley had calmed down enough and thought it would be a good idea to phone their neighbors to let them know what had happened and also where their horse was. In relating the events on the phone, it was the first time that Shirley remembered her view through the trees of the cave high up near the crest of the mountain.

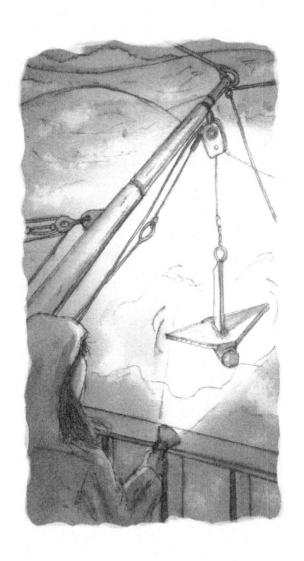

CHAPTER 2

Shirley sat on the big rock overlooking the wharf and inlet. Her mother had phoned from Comox saying that they would be arriving back home that evening. The trip would take three hours so Shirley had a good while to mull over the hunting trip she and her father had taken a few days before. The vision of the cave in the top of the mountain kept crowding her thoughts but always her mind would race back to the image of her father crumpled against the tree.

For her father's homecoming, Shirley had brushed her long black hair and put it in braids, the way he liked it, rather than her usual pony tail. She put on a skirt and nice top over her lithe fourteen year old tomboyish figure, knowing that this would please her father even more so.

A distant growl of tires over the stony dirt road caused a smile to cross her ruddy but pretty face. She turned her head to see the headlights wending their way toward the house.

Shirley saw her father emerge from the van with crutches under his shoulders and a bandage around his head. She jumped off the rock and raced to him. It was good to have him home. They all went into the house and sat by the fire that illuminated each face with a flickering resonance.

For the next couple of days, the family began organizing for the opening of the commercial fishing season.

"The season for chum salmon is opening next week and I will not be able to go for the first part," said her dad. "Shirley, you and Molly will have to go out with the deck hands. You'll miss a bit of school. We will let the school know of the circumstances and I'm sure they'll understand."

The girls had been out often with their dad and were familiar with the boat and the job that would be required of them. Luckily, one of the brothers, Chris, had his skipper's license and was well-suited for such an occasion.

"Should we begin to outfit the boat tomorrow?" Shirley asked.

"Yes, that would be a good idea," answered her father. "I'll get in touch with Chris and Thom right now so they can bring their truck tomorrow morning and the four of you can head over to the boat in Tahsis. Your mother will start organizing the food for you."

It was a comfort to Shirley feeling that things were beginning to get back to normal. Her father's voice became more business like now that he was talking about the boat and their livelihood.

The brothers arrived at seven o'clock the next morning and Shirley's mother had laid out a nice breakfast before they took off to the boat.

"Remember that both the girdy and spool mechanisms need to be cleaned and greased," reminded her dad while enjoying a slice of bacon. "Look at the level of oil in the crank case in the engine. Also the compression needs to be checked."

Both Shirley and her sister nodded, mumbling, "Okay," through their mouthful of eggs and hash browns.

It took four days of running back and forth from the boat to outfit it and make sure that all the mechanical workings were in order.

Two days before the season opened, the four headed for the last time to Tahsis with a truck full of food and high spirits. It would take them a day to position the boat five to ten miles offshore out from Kyuquot Sound into the open Pacific Ocean. The weather was mild and the rolling swells peaked at about ten feet. The boat was a fifty foot troller with a strong wooden hull. In the wheel house, the four of them easily had enough room to sit comfortably to eat the dinner that Thom had prepared in the galley.

"What time does the season start?" asked Shirley, knowing full well but just wanting to get a conversation started with the two brothers, who don't like to talk much.

"Eight o'clock in the morning," blurted Thom, knowing what Shirley was up to.

From then until bedtime, the chitchatting didn't cease. Chris finally looked at the clock and said, "Work tomorrow." With that, they trundled off to bed, leaving Chris to stay up for the first watch.

At the start of the season the next morning, the wind had picked up but it still looked to be a good day for a catch. Thom had made a breakfast before the deckhands got to work. As Thom doled out the mainline from the spool, the girls quickly attached a lure and hook to every two fathoms of length. There would be about twelve hooks on each mainline. This kept Shirley and her sister busy as there were four spools of line to be unwound off the stern. There was no time to daydream. By midday, the wind was blowing at fifteen knots and the swells were becoming choppy. Still, it was good fishing weather.

Thom yelled, "Start winding in the first line. I can see some flashes out there. I think we may be into some pay dirt."

Molly turned on the motor to wind in the first spool of line while Shirley stood at the stern to gather in the catch off the hooks.

Shirley, while removing the fish from the hooks, sliced their gills to bleed them. This took a good sharp knife and a sure hand. Later, the fish were dressed, leaving the heads still on and packed into ice until delivered to the packing house. Shirley was so used to the routine that she began to daydream, though still aware enough not to jeopardize her safety.

"I wonder if the cave is an old first nation's burial location?" she mused. "Dad took me to a burial site on a small island near

Esperanza. The bodies were buried in what people call bentwood cedar boxes and they were piled high under an overhanging cleft. It was very quiet in that gully. You could almost hear the bones in those boxes talking."

"Shirley, pay attention to what you're doing. You almost cut your hand," screeched Molly.

Shirley automatically looked down at her hand, realizing she had nicked it, but it wasn't bad.

"I must be more careful," she admonished herself.

Four days of fishing came and went without any more mishaps. The ice boxes were filling up. Their catch was good.

That evening, Chris said the radio forecast mentioned a storm was brewing from the southeast. "If it gets too rough, we might have to use the stabilizers," he went on. "It will be Thom's watch so he will let us know. We should go to bed soon as it might be a long night."

In the middle of her sound sleep, Shirley woke to a slamming blow by the side of her head and then a prolonged vibration. Before she could think, "What was that?" another punctuated crash ravaged her. She scrambled out of bed and whipped her cloths on over her nightgown. She met Molly in the galley and both headed outside. Shirley leaned hard on the door and it opened, but the wind threw her back against the opposite wall and the door slammed shut, wedging itself against the frame.

"Molly, grab the safety harnesses from the galley. I'll try to pry open the door with a crowbar and then slip the end of the harness to the cable outside," bellowed Shirley.

The words were almost lost in the clattering and howling outside but Molly understood her sister's nervous antics. While Molly went to find the harnesses, Shirley looked for the tool she needed by the fire extinguisher. They both arrived back at the same time and slipped on their gear. Shirley pried in between the jam and door. It opened slightly, enough for Molly to slip her hand through and attach both harness ends. Shirley gave one big yank on the bar and the wind caught both of them squarely in the face.

Shirley pushed her way out, followed by her sister, inching their way to the wheelhouse along the narrow walkway beside the gunnels. Their safety gear kept them from being washed over the side by the battering waves. The pelting spray stung Shirley's face but through her watering eyes she saw safety approaching. Thom had been watching for them from inside cabin and opened the door quickly, hauling the girls in. Wet and slightly disorientated, Shirley quickly gained her composure.

Chris managed to cry out while pulling on the wheel, "We need to put down the stabilizers before a large swell hits and swamps us. I've been trying to keep the bow into the oncoming waves but the wind is so changeable that it constantly tries to turn us about. Shirley, you and Thom can do that while Molly helps me with radar and compass readings."

Thom turned to Shirley and said, "How is your watch doing? Are we synchronized?"

"I've got ten after two," replied Shirley.

"Okay, we're ready to go. We will lower at two fifteen on the dot," said Thom, motioning with his hand.

The two went out of opposite doors of the wheel house as the stabilizers needed to be lowered simultaneously. Molly opened the door for Shirley and again the wind raged whipping her hair about her face. She was able to clip her safety gear back on to the cable. With the storm pinning her against the cabin, she managed to wend her way toward the stern. She stopped at the spar and looked at her watch. "Five, four, three, two, one," she counted, and then started to lower the boom.

She had done this exercise repeatedly until she could do it blindfolded. It was now time to let out the cable that the stabilizer hung on. She heard a muffled splash and then the boat shuddered as the cable tightened. The violent pitching ceased, allowing the craft to roll controllably with the choppy swells. Turning, Shirley inched her way back. Molly opened the door for her and she slipped her way in.

Shirley turned to Thom, who had already arrived back. "It's about time," she joked.

The four mates had a laugh and settled down to head for safer waters. Chris pointed the vessel due east back to Kyuquot Sound, Tahsis and home. They arrived in the shelter of the inlet early that morning, all a bit frayed but in good spirits. Shirley was able to let her mind wander over her recent adventures, ending up dwelling once again on the cave high on the mountain.

CHAPTER 3

"Dad, have you ever heard of a cave on the mountain above the path where you fell?" Shirley asked. "While I was pulling you up to safety, I happened to look up through the trees and from a certain angle I saw what looked like a hole near the top."

Shirley's father thought for a moment. "No, I haven't. Maybe you can ask some of your friends at school in case any of them have an idea."

In the days that followed, Shirley asked her friends questions about the mountain and the cave. She was anxious to know more about any First Nations' myths and legends. No one had heard that there was a cave in that particular mountain, though they gave her some history of the local First Nations People. They said that "Nuu-chah-nulth" was the name of a group of related peoples that lived in the general region of West Vancouver Island. They were known to have lived there for at least five thousand years. The local ancestral band was recognized as the "Deer People". The people survived on the sea as fishermen and whalers. They would gather berries and roots to supplement their diet. Huge cedar dugout canoes carried the hunters out to the open sea where they would search for and kill the whale with harpoons.

Shirley's imagination swelled with images of what she might find in her secret cavern. She felt compelled to ask her parents if she could use spring break to take a solitary climb up into the mountains and see if what she saw was actually a cave.

That night over supper, Shirley looked up from her plate full of stir-fry and took a deep breath.

"Mom and Dad, I've been thinking a lot about the cave that I saw up in the mountains and can't seem to get it out of my mind," she began. "I was wondering, could I go up there by myself on spring break and do a bit of exploring? I know you might think I'm a bit young but I know I'd be all right. Dad, you and I have done a lot of climbing with the mountaineering club and I know my knots and gear really well. It would be good for me to do that."

There was a long silence with her father and mother looking at each other.

"We'll think about it. We trust that you're capable but there will be questions that will nag us," her mother answered. "So we can't give you an answer right away. We will let you know soon."

Shirley felt a bit let down at first but realized at the same time, her parents needed to feel comfortable with the idea. She decided not to nag and left it up to them to come to her when they were ready.

The next few weeks were filled with school and Shirley would practice climbing with the mountaineering club without her father, who was now able to go out fishing with Chris and Thom but not much more. She still had not heard anything from her parents about her request and was feeling that they may have forgotten.

"Shirley," announced her father one evening.

She looked up from the book she was reading. She squirmed in her seat on the coach and her heart felt as though it were in her throat.

"Your mother and I have not gotten back to you until now because we wanted to do some research on the computer," continued her father. "We found on the web a device that uses the global positioning system for communication and finding locations. Let's say you were up in the mountains and needed to get in touch with us, all you would have to do is enter our identification number into your handset and a signal would bounce off a satellite to find our handset, then we could talk or communicate by text message. It will also let us know your exact location."

"Wow!" exclaimed Shirley, feeling more relaxed.

"Do you think that we can get one?" she exploded more excitedly.

"We sent for it and it's already here," her father answered in a quieting voice. "We can try it out in the next couple of days and if it works, your mother and I have decided that you can go on your trek."

"Thank you Mom and Dad," their daughter replied with affection, giving each of her parents a hug.

Over the next couple of weeks and up to the beginning of spring break, Shirley began sorting all the things in her mind that she needed to do to prepare herself for the hike. She needed to make sure that she had plenty of good strong rope and climbing gear. Along with her bug lamp, she would also take some candles and matches. Since she was going to explore a cave, it was essential that she had a large role of tough lightweight string. The list went on until she was sure that she had everything covered.

"Time for dinner," Mom yelled up stairs to the two girls.

Shirley and her sister thumped down the steps and raced toward the kitchen.

"I made your favorite, Shirley. It will help you on your way tomorrow morning," offered her mother.

"Thank you, Mom."

Shirley's enthusiasm spilled over as she wolfed down the steak, peas and mash potatoes.

"Cherry pie is my favorite. Mom knows me too well," she thought, bubbling over inside.

"Did you remember the moose jerky and the fruit leather?" Mom asked.

"Yes, I did. Thanks Mom," she answered. "I think I will head on up stairs to get a good night sleep. See you early tomorrow morning."

"Good night," the other three chirped.

Shirley climbed the stairs with an urgency she had never felt. She looked through her pack again to make sure that she hadn't left anything out.

"Everything's there. I guess I'd better go to bed," she thought.

She put on her night gown and turned off the lights. She looked out her window, but except for the splotch of light cast from the kitchen, it was totally dark. She scanned the woods beyond the clearing.

"What was that?" she said aloud to herself.

Her eyes caught a vacant shape in the trees. She knew that while hunting, seeing a void meant that an animal was usually there standing stalk still. Shirley, not staring directly at the shape, held her breath and the silhouette began to move in and behind the trees. It was a young two-point buck.

"What's a deer doing there moving around when it should be sleeping?" she wondered.

Shirley turned away puzzled. She got into bed still wondering. Finally, with the lingering visions of the cave behind dreaming eyes, sleep overtook her.

CHAPTER 4

The air outside was nippy and the ground underfoot crunched as Shirley began wending her way up the slope near their home. Here and there, the crocuses had begun popping up, pushing their way through the icy earth. The pussy willows opened softly, inviting a venturing hand for a caress. She opened her lungs to the fresh crackling air as her home began to recede in the distance.

Shirley, remembering the smiles on her parents' faces as she departed, left her reflecting. "I sure love my family." Her brown eyes sparkled with the thought of them.

"I will discover something new and make my parents proud," she mused.

It seemed like hours before the sun began to pierce the morning fog, shooting beams at the mountains, lighting up the towering peaks, and soon to be warming Shirley's bitten cheeks.

"I have about two hours to go before I can start looking for the cave," she thought. "I wonder if I will be able to see the passage through the trees and view the cave beyond or if there will be some shift in the boughs to block my vision."

Shirley thought often about this possibility but it never deterred her enthusiasm.

On either side of the path, she glimpsed new shoots of stinging nettles and sword ferns. She thought about how wonderful they tasted as an early spring delicacy. The smell of wild French mint occasionally tickled her nostrils as a soft warming breeze slid by and then sped away.

At first, Shirley's pack felt heavy and unwieldy, but as she got closer to the spot where her father had fallen, it was almost as though she carried no burden.

"It should be just around the bend in the path," she said to herself. "I will probably have to use the rope again to lower myself down to the tree."

She had walked a couple of hundred meters and looked down at the tree and the void dropping away. She looked to her left, viewing the solid wall of forest between her and the mountain beyond.

She had strapped the rope to the outside of her pack for easy access. Inside, she found a carabiner that would help her repel down to where her father had fallen. Shirley tied the rope to the same tree as before and started descending.

"It's way easier when you come prepared," she thought.

As she climbed down closer to the tree, Shirley kept raising her eyes in hopes that she would find the opening through the trees. She then stood at the gnarled trunk peering up.

"Nothing," she said aloud. "Maybe if I climb back up I'll see it from a different angle."

Shirley tried a few times up and down but to no avail.

"Maybe it was just a dream," she reflected. "I was pretty tired."

As she turned to trudge up the slope again, Shirley caught something in the corner of her eye. She stopped, afraid to look at it straight on, thinking it could be a dark spot that would simply vanish. Slowly, she turned her face towards the opening in the trees. It did not vanish. She looked keenly and saw that there was an outcropping of rock just below what looked to be an opening. If she shifted the angle of her line of sight, it shielded the cave from view.

"How am I to find that point on the mountain when I can only see the cave from here through the tiny opening in the forest? No wonder no one knew about it," she mused.

Shirley pulled out her compass and took a bearing.

"The cave is thirteen degrees from the northwest. The sun will be at my back but will move to my left as the day passes," she calculated.

She looked through the gap in the trees to study the shape and colour of the rock, recording the image firmly in her mind before she climbed back up the embankment for the last time.

What faced Shirley now was a steep climb up through the dense forest of evergreens. She had to make sure that the sun stayed at her back. Shooting a glance backwards every now and then, she would catch a glimpse of the orb trying to penetrate the thickening boughs. A stone wall suddenly jutted up before her, impeding her progress.

"I need to find a way straight to the top of this outcropping without straying from my line of direction, otherwise I will lose my bearings."

The girl grasped at the stony face and found the rock to be rotten. It crumbled when any force was applied to it.

"Where do I go?" She was speaking aloud now.

She side-stepped and saw a small gully just to the side of a large tree, which blocked her view.

"It winds its way to the top and the rock looks sound."

Slowly, she wended her way upwards. Even in the cold, droplets of sweat stung her eyes. The pack felt heavy in the gloomy overgrowth.

"Maybe I shouldn't have taken so much, but I'll be all right. I'm about half way up and it's not as steep."

When Shirley reached the top of the rock formation, she sat down and removed the pack. Opening a zipper on the side, she reached in and fumbled around for a plastic bag and pulled it out. She took a bite off a small bit of dried venison. The jerky momentarily staved off her hunger but she would eat a meal once she broke through the gnarled forest higher up. After being confronted with a few more stony abutments and twisted undergrowth, she could see that the bush seemed to be thinning out. She had probably climbed at least a couple of thousand vertical feet since morning.

"The tree line must be getting near. The growth is becoming more sparse and smaller."

The weight on her back seemed to get easier as the daylight began filtering through the thinning trees. Then out of the corner of her eye she caught the flashing tail of a deer. It disappeared just as she turned her head to look for it. Shirley was drawn to the spot where the deer had vanished. There she saw a trail that seemed to lead up in the direction that she wanted to go. Forgetting her desire to continue climbing up in a straight line, she began following the track. It eventually led her out into the open with a clear view of the mountain above. She basked in the warmth of the sun as she scanned the mountain top looking for a certain colour and formation. It was nowhere to be seen.

She climbed up onto a large boulder; took out the sandwich that she had prepared at home, and looked up again at the vastness of the mountain.

"Will I find my cave?" she wondered. "It almost seems hopeless with so many shapes and colours up there."

"There's that deer again," she said in an excited voice while squinting her eyes, making out the far away silhouette. "Maybe I should follow it."

Shirley slid off the rock and found the track again that the deer was taking. She found it easy climbing as the trail found the simplest way around obstacles and over rocks. Every now and then, she would spot the animal far ahead, waiting as if he were making sure that she was following.

The sun began stretching toward the horizon. She could see the distant shore of the inlet that she lived on. Her heart though was too much into the adventure to feel at all homesick. The sighting of her four legged companion seemed to be more frequent as she trudged up the steeper slope nearing the top of the mountain.

Scanning the nearby rocks, she became aware of something familiar.

"There it is," she whispered, hardly able to believe her eyes. "The cave must be just behind that overhang. There's my friend again." Her heart was pounding now as she excitedly scurried toward her goal, sometimes slipping on loose gravel, not caring about the footing.

"The cave has to be there," she muttered, rounding a corner on the path.

It was there tucked in behind two large boulders, not very big but large enough for a couple of people to crawl through together. Shirley removed her pack and crept closer to the opening. She saw some tracks leading inside and coming back out. Some were hoofed and others too small and old to make out. A set of clawed paw prints still seemingly fresh in the mud led into the darkness but did not reemerge. A chill climbed up the middle of her back, reaching a clenched mouth that grew tighter as she pondered momentarily her mission.

Shirley moved away from the opening, which seemed to be drawing her inside. "I'm not ready to go in," she thought. "The sun is going down. I'd better gather some firewood, pitch the tent and see how I feel in the morning."

By the time the sun set, Shirley had found a comfortable place away from the cave and whatever might find its way out during the night. She had eaten and decided to sit up for a while to enjoy the warmth of the fire, listening to the silence of the mountain and stars.

The stillness was broken by the snap of a twig not far away. Shirley snapped her head around. There was nothing. Again, a sound shattered the night. This came from closer. The fire light jumped and leaped, periodically illuminating an animal slowly creeping closer to the encampment. To her relief, it was the deer that she had kept spotting on the way up to the cave.

When Shirley's anxiety had subsided enough, she said softly to the welcome intruder, "Don't be uneasy."

The deer slowly crept closer. The fire crackled and spit an ember out. The deer jumped with its ears pinned back, yet still inched forward.

"My name is Shirley", said the girl in a loud whisper. "I think that I saw you down by my home and later on coming up the mountain."

The deer's ears shifted forward and his nose began to twitch. His spikes were that of a yearling coming into velvet. He seemed healthy with a pelt that was well cared for.

The climb that day was beginning to have an effect on Shirley, even though the presence of the deer intrigued and excited her.

"I don't want to be a party pooper but I need to hit the sack," she said aloud, as much to herself as to the deer. "Are you going to be here in the morning?"

The deer shifted and stomped his hoof as if to say, "Good night."

Shirley crawled into her tent and was soon asleep.

CHAPTER 5

Shirley awoke to the sound of loud snuffling close to her head on the outside of the tent. A shadow projected itself on the lightweight fabric stretching over her.

"Is that you, my friend?"

The shadow jumped, startled by the impromptu voice. It still came closer, sniffing.

"Are you trying to tell me that it's time to get up and begin the day?"

This time the animal didn't budge. Shirley could see the silhouette of his tail wagging swiftly like a cuddly lap dog. The sleepy girl crawled out of her sleeping bag, slipped on her clothes and opened the flap to the warm sun that caressed her face. She looked around and found the deer looking intently at her. She smiled.

"It looks like you want to be around me," she said. "Can I give you a name? I remember a book that my father had read to us girls and there was a lion in it by the name of Tyke. Shall I call you that?"

Tyke cocked his ears forward and snorted.

"Then it's settled."

Shirley quickly built herself a fire to bake some trail bread that she had wound around a stick. It was a good time to think about what she would do next. Then she remembered the tracks going into the cave but not coming out. While the bread cooked propped up over the fire, Shirley went over to the cave and looked at the mud. A set of the clawed prints left the cave. A chill crawled up her spine.

"The animal must have come back out during the night. It looks like the tracks of a cougar," she whispered, almost too faint for her own ears.

Shirley put the thought out of her mind and started looking for a sturdy bush or small sapling that she would be able to attach the string she had brought. A few feet away from the cave opening stood a sturdy shrub that would suit her purpose. Shirley packed her belongings, put out the fire and went to the cave where she securely tied on the end of the string to the plant and stood before the mouth of the cave. She could feel a slight breeze on her face coming from within. Tyke had crept up tentatively from behind.

"Are you coming with me, Tyke?" she asked. The deer pawed the ground. "Okay, we're in this together."

She put a fresh candle into the bug lamp and lit it. She ducked her head and ventured inside. Tyke followed.

She thought of the tracks again. "If there was anything to be frightened of inside, Tyke would be able to sense it and wouldn't follow me," she whispered to herself, finally relieving the dread she felt within.

The darkness was still and the lamp barely penetrated the solitude. A musty odor filled with decay and dampness pierced her innermost person. The sound of sharp hooves striking loose gravel behind her was a warm reminder of companionship Shirley needed to feel so desperately in this depraved enclosure. She let out the string, careful not to get it snagged on anything for fear of it snapping. Here and there, the sounds of water dripping and unseen feet pattered to the left and right of her. It was a place full of life but not like anyone knew. Tyke stayed close behind her while they crept deeper into the cavern. The light from the entrance was now completely gone and to go one way or the other seemed irrelevant. The only thing that gave Shirley a discernible direction to go in was the constant but subtle breeze against her cheeks. She would follow this in the hopes that it would eventually lead the two of them to an outside entrance.

"Tyke, I can barely make out the path. It seems to split in two directions. Should we take the right or the left?"

The opening to the right seemed larger so she decided to take it. They walked a little but then she could not feel the draft.

"I think we went the wrong way."

Tyke snorted.

"Yes, I would agree with you," she said to her friend.

They backtracked and Shirley wound up the spent string as they went. Again, the scuttling of feet resumed around them.

"I wish I knew what little animals were making all the noise."

She shined the light around but the beam did not illuminate anything.

Back at the fork, Shirley pointed the light down at the other opening.

"I will have to shove the pack in first and then squirm on my belly to get through. Tyke, we will have to figure out how to get you through."

The girl blew out the bug lamp and her hands began fumbling in the dark, pushing the pack through the opening along with the lamp. On her front, Shirley inched her way, scratching her bare stomach as she went. She made sure that the string didn't get caught underneath her. Once she was on the other side, her fingers reached for the matches in her pack and lit the lamp. Tyke had gotten down on his haunches, wedging his way through. Shirley had to grab hold of one of his legs and pull. Tyke let out a slight squeal but then was all the way through to the other side. He lay for a moment panting, his tongue lolling out to one side.

"This must be very hard for you. I don't imagine that you have ever done this before."

Tyke's eyes rolled up and met Shirley's. It was the first time they had made eye contact. They both sat transfixed for a few minutes and then got to their feet.

"We should move on. I can feel the air flow once again. We must be on the right course," she said with great confidence.

Shirley had lost all track of time. She could not tell the difference between a minute and an hour. She thought that they must have been in the cave for quite a while as she was beginning feel sleepy and hungry. She pointed the lamp to the watch on her arm.

"It's later than I thought. Let's move on a bit further and then we can have a bite to eat. I hope you like trail bread because that's about all I have for you."

Tyke grunted softly. They moved on, following the puff of air that wafted intermittently. The creatures of the cave again began making their almost inaudible noise and every now and then, a flapping would come close to Shirley's ears. She didn't fear the bats as they were always very careful not to hit anything in the dark using their sonar. She squirmed a bit at the thought of the other unseen creatures that seemed to be following them with their eyes constantly on her.

"Stop these thoughts," she muttered to herself. "This is all in your imagination. You're getting tired."

She became aware that the twine had almost run out. The dread of the cave inhabitants was nothing compared to the fear that her link to back home was ending as the ball gave out. If she needed to be found, there was no way that her GPS would ever work inside this dark hole. Terror gripped her body. She tried to speak to Tyke but all that came out was a pinched squeal. She had thought that the string would be long enough. After she had something to eat and a sleep, she could always retrace her steps by following the string back home, but then, "I will have failed."

Her body still quaking, Shirley decided to take the string to its end. This won't be fatal, she thought. The two inched on, the lamp swaying back and forth.

"What's that?"

Shirley purposely made the torch swing in an ark.

"There it is again. A corner of something," she whispered to her friend.

The cord had played out. She looked around for a large rock to place on top of the string before she went any further to investigate the abnormal apparition in the beam of light.

Stepping closer, the lamp illuminated more square corners and flat surfaces. She could see boxes piled on top of each other. Some of them had toppled over and were broken.

"Tyke, this reminds me of the burial caskets that Dad and I saw near Esperanza," she said.

They crept closer. Shirley could see that from some of the broken boxes, bones and tattered blankets had spilled out and that they were the same type of bent cedar boxes that she and her father had discovered a few years earlier. The light bounced eerily, casting undulating shadows on implements and tools placed in with the corpses. One box stood out from the rest. It was elaborately painted with scenes of trees, animals and a mountain.

Shirley got down on her knees and focused the beam closer.

"This looks like the Golden Hinde, the highest mountain on Vancouver Island," she said, pointing to the image. "There is also a figure of a deer. What does this all mean? It looks like there's a story to this. I'll have to figure it out."

She looked inside the container's splintered end, noticing a skull toward the back. Scattered about the other bones and frayed red blanket were tools for fishing and hunting. A beautiful obsidian knife was sheathed in a rotted leather pouch, which at one time could have looked elegant with abalone shell pieces sewn to it. Almost falling out was a bow and arrow meant for hunting sea otters. Also eloquently carved was a barbed bone point used as a harpoon.

There were other caskets with painted designs but Shirley kept shining the light back onto the mountain scene. There was something about it she couldn't let go of.

33

Shirley looked back inside the box that interested her. The beam of light played on the skull, casting eerie shadows. She looked closely at the teeth and saw that they were not at all worn.

"They could only be the teeth of a young person," she thought.

"This person must have been a young boy with all the tools a man would have used," she divulged in an exuberant but quiet voice. "What happened to him? Do the paintings somehow say something about his life?"

Shirley saw Tyke in the shadows lying down.

"You're right. We need to have a bite to eat and then have a rest. I am definitely getting tired."

She took out the trail bread and, leaning over, she gave some to her friend. He sniffed it and happily took it from her outstretched hand. Shirley fished in her pack and dug out some jerky to eat with her bread. She opened her water bottle and drank slowly.

"There isn't much left so I'd better take it easy."

She got out the ground tarpaulin, unrolled her sleeping bag, and her eyes were shut immediately as she slipped in.

Her eyes opened suddenly. It was pitch-black but she was woken from a deep dream. In it, she was falling from the top of a mountain, the same one from the painting on the side of the casket. There was a feeling of floating with a sense of euphoria and that of never touching the ground. She looked down at her body and realized that she was not looking at a girl's body but that of a boy. A deer seemed to be watching her fall from a long distance away standing near the peak of the mountain. Her vision was crystal clear, where all shapes and colors were vivid. She blinked her eyes and, seeing the darkness again, reached for the bug lamp.

When lit, she saw her friend in the shadows.

"We need to move on. Which way should we go? The water is almost gone and we've run out of string."

Shirley packed her bag and sat back against the cave wall. She could feel the slight breeze against her face. and hear a distant whooshing sound she had not heard before. She must have been too excited after discovering the boxes that she was not aware of the intermittent hum that was almost inaudible under the constant ringing in her ears.

Turning to Tyke, who was still lurking in the shadows, she said, "Let's go. There might be an end to this gloom close by."

Tyke's ears shot forward as he stood up. The two followed the beam from the lamp and the soft breeze that carried the distant sound. Moments later, Shirley could see a faint glow that grew in intensity with each advancing step. Rounding a bend in the cave, a blast of light pierced her pupils, making her eyes squint with pain and a deafening explosion of noise that almost threw her off balance. Before them, the cave opening stood gaping as though they were perched on the tongue of a giant who was venting with a roar. A water fall spilled out from above and the giant wept from a sadness that would never be quenched.

Shirley stepped into the effervescent light, which engulfed her and made her eyes water. She looked through the spray and saw the Pacific Ocean in the distance. She ventured out further onto the ledge at the cave's mouth but Tyke was more apprehensive and stayed well back from the opening.

Shirley looked over the outcrop and saw that it was a good forty feet down to some solid ground. She could make it if she were to inch over to the right of the fall on the shelf that protruded from the cave.

"What about Tyke? How would I get him down?" she wondered.

CHAPTER 6

Shirley stood behind the fall for a few moments feeling the spray against her body and consuming the freshness she so craved. The sun was at the back of the mountain that she and Tyke had just walked through but it shone on the peaks that rimmed the sea in the distance. When she finally felt refreshed, she turned to the right and began studying the rock that jutted out, forming a natural arc around the cascading water.

"If I use that rock to anchor a carabiner, from there the ground appears to slope further down than forty feet," she mused. "It looks though that is the only place I can climb down and the rock doesn't look rotten."

Again, she thought about Tyke. Almost before the dilemma had jelled in her mind, she had reached for the rope tethered to the back pack and began fashioning a harness using it and her jacket.

Tyke, who had not stepped out from the mouth of the cave, cocked his ears forward as he watched his companion's hands do strange things with a vine and her outer skin. As Shirley advanced toward him with an outstretched hand holding this device, the deer's ears flattened on the back of his neck. This was only the second time that the girl and deer had touched. Remembering that first experience, Tyke felt apprehensive and fear welled in his eyes.

"Tyke, I'm not going to hurt you," she cooed.

Her gentle voice softened the look in his eyes. She put her arms around his body. He flinched but accepted her embrace. It was a matter of quickly tying the knots and Tyke was securely in the tackle. She left him to get used to his new appendage while she climbed over the rock face to the spot where she had thought it best to hammer in the spike. She attached a carabiner to the secured spike, threaded the end of a rope through and pulled it to the deer. Shirley tied a special knot to the harness that could be released remotely. She tenderly led the deer over to the ledge. Pulling the rope taught, Tyke began to lift into the air, swinging under where the spike held fast. He began kicking, the fear returning this time to his whole body, but before he was fully aware of his plight, his hooves landed safely on the solid ground below. With a quick jerk of her hand, Shirley loosened the knot on the harness.

Once he settled, Tyke looked up to see where his companion was. She was already half way down the cliff, kicking out from the wall as she repelled.

Shirley rolled up the rope and secured it to the outside of her pack. They stood side by side, looking down the slope and measuring the easiest way to the bottom. The cold on the west side of the mountain bit through her shirt. Putting on her coat, she strained to find the faintest hint of a trail.

"There, that's the best way to go," she said out loud, pointing a finger.

The adventurers slid on the loose shale below the falls until they reached the track. They were close to the tree line now, yet still able to view the top of the forest as seen from the eyes of an eagle. Shirley let Tyke go ahead of her as it was easier for him to find the better footing. As they descended, maneuvering around the boulders and stunted trees, it became less precarious. Soon the fairy tale trees turned into giants overhead and the pathway meandered on a mild slope downwards.

Their journey led them into forested glades with a growing harvest of fiddle-heads and stinging nettles. Shirley put on some gloves and began picking the savory greens. Tyke browsed on the sparse grass that was left over from the fall before. From the coming of the spring crop, he found new shoots popping up here and there that quenched his appetite.

After filling a small portion of her pack with her morsels, she pointed to an out-cropping beyond the wooded perimeter.

"We need to get to those rocks to see where we need to go next."

Tyke looked up from his meal and shivered.

She began walking and this was the deer's signal to follow. He trotted to catch up and made a whining noise. Shirley looked back and smiled. "I would feel alone without you as well."

Her smile quickly turned to a grimace when a crashing clamor broke the silence. Just ahead through the bush, a black splotch appeared and then disappeared. Behind them, a squalling from two directions lashed out from beyond the meadow.

"Tyke, run to the right and get away from between the mother and her cubs," shrieked Shirley.

Out of the corner of her eye, the black shape reappeared, this time moving fast gaining on the two. She then noticed the squabbling brood. Now she and Tyke bolted in another direction, hoping to confuse the mother. The bear stopped dead, looking first at her babies and then at the intruders. She snorted her rage and loped over to her offspring.

"Wow! That was a close call. We walked right in between them."

They stood panting, watching to make sure that the mother didn't change her mind and double back. They didn't move until the crashing of the animals dwindled away.

Cautiously, they again began moving towards the grade that would eventually lead to a good view point.

Shirley found some solid footing on the pillar of rock and studied the panorama.

"There, that's what I saw in my dream in the cave and on the box," she said excitedly.

A huge mountain loomed in the distance. Snow was still stubbornly covering its surface.

"Winter is still on top there," she thought, trying to stifle the shudder growing inside her. "Tyke, that's where we're heading. I think it's called the Golden Hinde," she said aloud but in a lowered voice. Shirley was in awe of the spectacle before her and the formidable task that she felt lay in front of her.

Tyke could feel the tension in the girl. He came close and nuzzled her hand.

"Yes, you feel it too, don't you?"

They stood motionless, both knowing what was ahead.

The sun by this time had risen up above the peak behind them, warming their backs. Once again, the spirit for adventure rose in their bodies as they began to climb back down from their lookout. As the mid-morning heat touched each dew-covered leaf, a spiral of steam rose and collected into a mist, engulfing the ground where they walked.

The adventurers headed on through glades of alder and willow, looking for patches of sunlight to step into and warm themselves. In the distance, Shirley could hear the thunder of the spring runoff. They heard sounds like laughter and a full orchestra playing a Strauss waltz amongst the bellowing roar. They hiked over fallen trees and thick bush heading towards the clamor. A crumbling bank emerged before them.

"I'm hungry. How about you, Tyke? This looks like a good place to rest and have a bite to eat," she said as she plunked herself down on a fallen log. "We can also figure out the best way to go. The river is swollen and it looks impassible here."

Shirley removed the greens she had collected and a morsel of jerky from her pack. While Tyke ate around the fringes of their resting spot, the girl gathered dried moss and kindling for a small fire to boil the stinging nettle and fiddle-heads. When the water was simmering, she dumped in her cache along with the venison.

The aroma rose to Shirley's nostrils, creating a stinging sensation under her ears. Tyke lifted his head, not liking the smell of the meat.

"We should walk along the shore as it seems to be heading toward our mountain," she blurted out with a mouthful.

She lay back for a moment and then was on her feet.

"Come on, Tyke. The day is wasting."

The two climbed down to the river's edge heading upstream. It was easier to walk there than to climb over rotted stumps and thick brambles on the bank. The sun was fully on them, warming them as they went.

Suddenly, Shirley heard a thunderous crack up stream The deer bolted, his eyes glazed with fright.

CHAPTER 7

The rushing of water and pounding of wood against wood was deafening. A wall of broken tree trunks in an angry gnarled soup lunged toward Shirley. She had to get out of the gully to live. The deer tried but failed to scale the embankment and so was sucked in by the churning torrent. "An ice dam has broken upstream," she screamed. "Get on a log!" Her words were choked and swallowed by the bellowing tide.

Shirley had managed to grab onto to a root that stuck out from the embankment and slowly pulled herself up as the water kept trying to suck her down. She kicked her leg upwards and hooked it onto another root higher up. Twisted limbs and dense brush careened by, just missing her head as she hung upside down, desperately hanging on. With the weight of her pack pulling her down, she could still manage to inch her way up. Moments later, she lay panting on the bank. Shirley's eyes scanned the torrent but could see no sign of Tyke. She removed her pack and rolled over onto her back, looking into the tree tops not wanting to move.

When Shirley regained her breath, she again thought of her companion.

"Get up, Shirley, and look for your friend," she spoke aloud.

She got up slowly and began walking downstream, her eyes scouring the river's edge.

"Tyke," she yelled, but could barely hear her own voice.

Tears of exhaustion and fear rolled down her cheeks. "Where is he?" she muttered. There was no answer.

On she trudged, feeling desperate. "Look over there by that bobbing log," a voice urged inside of her.

Shirley's gaze was fixed on a small brown spot that would appear and then disappear. She ran over and looked down between two broken trees. There he was, wedged but above water.

"Hold on, Tyke. I'll get you out of there."

Shirley looked over the edge and realized that there was no footing. "If I could get down, there are some rocks large enough and high enough above the water that I could get on my belly to pull him out," she thought.

Looking into the thicket, Shirley saw a dead alder that maybe she could shove down. The girl charged over and began pushing and pulling at the tree, making it sway until, *crack*, it broke. The tree was dead and dried, but it was a heavy haul to bring back. She slid it over the brink and down to the shore, wedging the end between two boulders. The pole was propped at a good angle for her to slide down. The water level had dropped down to about normal but Tyke was still struggling to keep his head above the river.

He let out a muffled snort as Shirley climbed down. The rocks were a good size, which reassured her that she would not fall in. She saw that the log upstream was pushing and trapping the deer against the log downstream. Shirley got on her stomach and began pushing with one leg while her other leg and arms wrapped around the rocks securing her. The battered piece of wood slowly moved upstream and out toward the middle. Tyke began struggling and flaying with his hooves.

"Tyke, hold still. You might become entrapped again," she urged. "I will open the gap and help you out."

Tyke stopped kicking but his eyes were still frantic. The girl let go of the log once it was far enough away and then grabbed onto the deer under his front legs and pulled him out. They lay on the rocks exhausted.

Shirley spoke with a faltering breath, "Tyke we have to get up and climb out as soon as we can or we'll catch a chill."

They got up, Tyke in the front being pushed from behind. Shirley had to keep the deer from falling by propping him with her hands.

The top of the bank was a welcome respite for both of them. When they regained their strength, they headed back up to where Shirley had left her pack. On the way, she dug up some Oregon grape root since she was feeling the sniffles coming on.

"Tyke, we have to stop and build a fire. I'm cold and I think you are as well," she said with authority. "I'm going to make some tea with this plant and maybe you should try some, even though it tastes so bitter. It's good for what ails you."

Tyke began to walk in circles until he found a suitable spot to lie down. He knew his companion was going to make him more comfortable when he saw her with an armload of sticks and lichen.

The fire crackled noisily and the two sat transfixed. Their tired bodies ached and the moments turned to hours. The sun sank lower until it was obliterated by mountains that skirted the small valley. Afternoon noises turned to night murmurings before they realized it.

"Gosh, it's almost dark," Shirley announced with astonishment. "I wanted get further than we are but I guess we will have to stay here. There's water, we already have a fire going and I'm hungry."

Shirley found some branches that she used for a lean-to structure and cut some fir boughs to make the roof and flooring. She lashed a long pole between two trees to prop up the others.

"There, this will keep the rain off if need be. There's room for you too, Tyke."

The deer didn't pay much attention to his friend as he was still trying to keep warm and get the taste of the tea out of his mouth by munching on nearby grass.

Shirley still had some of the greens she had picked earlier so she made some more soup with that and the jerky from her pack.

A frost filled the air and her sleeping bag was a welcome comfort. Tyke decided to walk in circles again to find a snug place rather than try to stuff himself into the little space that Shirley had provided. The darkness was completely overtaken by a stillness that seeped into every hiding place in the forest. Shirley slept soundly, only waking now and again to stir the fire and put on more wood.

CHAPTER 8

Opening her eyes, Shirley could feel her slimy body quaking with a chill. The air in her nostrils slipped coolly in and out, filling her with the morning cold. The sun was low behind the surrounding mountain and would not begin to warm the forest for many hours. Tyke had found a spot close to her to sleep but now was awake and aware of something that stirred close by. Her ears picked up the sound now. She could feel her face slowly turning pale as she held her breath. A slow crunching and gurgling sound grew in intensity behind her lean-to.

"What's that?" she thought trembling.

She could see Tykes eyes were fixed on an object. Shirley grappled with her fear and finally turned around, looking through the boughs of her shelter. A low growl emerged from a fury mound as she moved to get a better look. The mass now had a head with a muzzle covered in red. More gnashing was heard as teeth cracked through, splintering bone and tearing at flesh. Behind the head, Shirley could see two tan stripes on a pelt of dark brown.

"A wolverine," she screeched as her hand shot out for a loose stick that was perched near the cooling embers of the fire.

The startled deer reared back, not so much from the carnivore but from Shirley's outburst. She was on her feet in a flash, stick in hand, rounding the corner of her shelter. The snarling beast turned to face her. He was going to protect his meal at all costs from this deafening creature. Shirley did not dare step backwards for fear of giving this beast the advantage. Tyke by this time had disappeared behind some trees near the river's edge.

Keeping her stick pointing at the marauder, Shirley began rolling up her sleeping bag and placing all her belongings into the back pack. She would not keep her eye off the menacing brute. He kept making angry guttural outbursts deep in his throat, keeping his ground. The standoff was vicious, each not knowing what the other would do.

Finally, the wolverine snatched up his meal and slunk back into the underbrush. Shirley stood, not wanting to turn her back on the place where he had melted into the woods. Her body was not shaking from the cold anymore but from her encounter.

"I didn't know that there were wolverines on Vancouver Island," she thought curiously. "I know that they live on the mainland. Maybe they've been island hoping over the years."

Once she got her composure and felt sure that the animal was gone, Shirley turned to look for Tyke.

"Where are you, my friend?" she pleaded, hoping he hadn't been frightened away.

Tyke momentarily revealed his whereabouts by letting out a low whimper. Shirley saw his tail flicking back and forth through the dense stand of trees. Slowly, the deer crept into the clearing, cautiously placing one foot out and then another.

Shirley smiled, well aware that she could have lost her companion forever.

By mid-morning, the sun had lifted itself above the surrounding peaks and bathed the travelers in a worm glow. Occasionally, Shirley would spot the mountain that was tugging on her. It was sometimes shrouded in haze but other times a brilliant beam was cast from the reflective snow cap. Their path would take them back and forth across the river depending upon the ease of travel.

Shirley had forgotten about the morning's confrontation as she walked spellbound in the surrounding splendor of nature.

"Tyke, why don't we rest for a spell on the rocks overlooking those falls," she said, pointing. "The climb is getting steeper the closer we get to the mountain."

They stood on the outcropping of rocks peering down on a dazzling pond.

"Look, I see some trout. Boy that would make a nice meal."

She saw one of the fish dart in under a boulder.

"I'm going to try to catch that fish," she told Tyke matter-of-factly.

Tyke watched with interest as Shirley stripped off her clothes, slid down over the face of the rock and gently stepped into the pool, not causing a ripple that would spook her quarry. Her breath was momentarily paralyzed from the icy clear water but soon she was completely under, swimming toward the rock where she had last seen the fish. She inserted her arm up past the elbow into a shelf under the rock. Her fingers felt around for the familiar slimy sensation of a fish's back.

"There it is," she mused.

Shirley extended her arm as far in as it would go, wedging the fish up against the innermost wall, pinning it to allow her fingers to slowly inch their way towards the head. She could tell it was a good sized trout as her thumb and forefinger pinched together, grappling the gills and immobilizing her catch.

She swam to the surface and boosted herself up. The fish wriggled violently while she struggled to climb back up to the top of her perch. Shirley took the doomed fish by the tail and slammed its head hard against the rock. It went limp.

"You must think I'm horrible," she said to Tyke sheepishly. "I didn't want it to flip and flop around suffering."

Tyke made a shrill rasping sound that came blowing out on his nostrils.

"Okay! I'm not really that bad," she scoffed.

Shirley dried herself with her sweater and put her clothes back on, which had been warming in the sun.

They climbed down from their ledge and she found a stick to hang the fish on.

"This will make a nice meal for a change," she said under her breath, still feeling the sting from Tyke's body language and accusing snort.

They skirted the swimming hole and climbed up the small fall. From there Shirley could see an opening to the landscape. There was thicker brush and fewer trees.

"Tyke, it looks like we're close to a lake."

With a few more steps, she came face to face with an overwhelming spectacle. Shirley's mouth dropped open in awe. She tried to speak but nothing came out. It was the mountain. It was glorious, frightening and divine all at once. The pinnacle was capped with snow and billowing clouds were being whisked about sometimes obliterating and sometimes showcasing its majesty. At the foot of this imposing peak was a broad body of water named by the local people as The Lake of Tears.

Tyke also seemed mesmerized at the scene before him. His ears were pushed forward in a quizzical manner. He would not lower his gaze but instead stood transfixed.

Finally, Shirley broke the spell and said, "We need to find a camping spot and have a good rest. We have a big day ahead of us tomorrow."

Tyke looked at the girl, his trance broken. The adventurers began wading through dense brush and marshy bogs, until their way was clear. The water in front of them was smooth without much of a swell. They could see the mountain clearly upside down with even an eagle being reflected in the contrasting scene.

"Let's try to make it over to that bit of land that's jutting out. It's a spot where we would have full view of the lake," Shirley urged.

The trudging was rough but they arrived unscathed by the brambles and broken snags. Shirley immediately set up camp and started gathering dry moss and sticks. A lot of driftwood had collected on the shore from past storms.

"We will be toasty warm tonight," she said while building the fire.

Tyke had already found his spot to lie down after his nightly ritual of prancing around in circles.

"You're funny Tyke," Shirley said warmly, smiling. "I wish it were as easy for me to find my bed after walking in circles."

The fire had died to coals low enough for her to prop the fish on a spit. Shirley's ears stung as the smell reached her nose and the anticipation of her biting into the fragrant flesh was the only thing on her mind.

Around them, the darkness had settled and the quiet had replaced the light. Once Shirley had eaten, she got up and walked to the shore. Tyke kept a close watch on her but she didn't go far.

She looked up at the stars and then down at the stars. There was no meeting of sky and land but it seemed all to be one. She began to feel her body floating outwards towards the middle, completely surrounded by the heavens. The euphoria felt timeless. It was the great meeting place of the spirit and she was a part of this divine scheme.

CHAPTER 9

Shirley shook the frost off her sleeping bag. She sat up and looked around. Tyke was nowhere to be seen. She called out but there were no familiar snorts or hoof beats reaching her ears through the crisp morning air. This was the first time that she felt alone.

"Tyke, where are you?" she pleaded.

Still there was nothing. Then the mountain before her took her attention. She felt even more remote. Shirley hadn't realized how much she depended on her friend for companionship.

"Why did he leave now?" she thought. "Is there something out there that I should be aware of?"

She looked around with more alertness. Her eyes searched the dense undergrowth and as far as she could see into the trees. Shadows danced as demons and gnarled stumps watched her warily like wild beasts in hiding.

"Stop it," she said, admonishing herself. "Think about what you need to do. Pack up your gear and get on your way."

Even though her words were enough to banish her paranoia, she still felt the emptiness without Tyke. Shirley's eyes looked up at the peak. She threw on her pack and, giving in to the lure of the mountain, she began to walk. Finding a path that bordered the lake was not an easy task with all the fallen timber to skirt around and bogs to negotiate. Patches of snow also impeded her progress so it took a couple of hours to reach the head waters.

After studying the terrain, she thought that at the beginning she would follow the stream, which headed up the slope. It was difficult to scrutinize much beyond the bottom of the mountain as there were obstacles in the way obstructing the view. At first it was easy walking, but soon it was not just a hike but a steep climb. She became winded and had to stop to catch her breath.

Shirley turned around to view where she had just come from.

"Wow," she thought. "I've done pretty well but I must continue on so I can reach the top by nightfall."

The smattering of snow had turned into small fields. Shirley skirted the slushy drifts, even though it meant traveling further. She was still below the tree line so she could not judge the direction she should go to reach the top. She would have to trust her instincts and go by the way of least resistance.

Shirley heard some footfalls behind her and spun around. She could just make out something in amongst the fir trees.

"Is that you, Tyke?" she ventured.

There were no familiar sounds.

"Don't be frightened," she said in a louder voice.

There was movement now and what Shirley hoped to be Tyke was not. A large set of velvet antlers appeared, much closer than she expected. From behind, a couple of lurking shadows materialized. The deer ran into an opening and spun to face his adversaries head on. The two wolves circled, trying to find an opening but the old bull had lived too many years to be out smarted by two fledgling carnivores. With a well-aimed hoof, the deer smacked one of the wolves on the hindquarters, sending it careening into a snow-covered bramble. The other was sent head over heals by a great thrust of a head butt. Stunned, the two predators ran off whimpering with their tails between their legs.

"Well done," Shirley said, relieved to be able to talk to someone.

The deer cocked his head as if to listen to the girl. It was almost as though the deer knew who she was and why she was standing there in his domain. The victor vanished with a twitch of his tail, leaving Shirley alone once again. The adventure was now beginning to weigh heavily on her. She thought of home and the warm bed that she would be getting into this evening if only she was there. Something drove her on, step by excruciating step.

"What is calling to me and why?" she wondered.

As the thinning trees gave way to an opening of the forest, Shirley could see that before her was a rock face that she would have to maneuver around to find an easier way up. She followed a trail that led to her right for about fifty meters until the cliff split off into a draw, which she would be able to go up. The slope was quite steep and there wasn't much snow to impede her climb. It wasn't long before she was on top of an overhang looking down.

"I think I can see the top but I will have to get back over to the left and head up from there," she thought with conviction.

On top of the precipice, the snow was deeper and more difficult to travel through. Finally, she made it to the spot where she had thought going straight up would lead her to the top. This incline was so shrouded in a dense fog that she could barely see around herself. Shirley struggled to stay on course but her only navigational tool was the sense of up and down. Her bag felt heavier and her breathing became labored as she ascended. She could feel the hardened and slippery ice under the newer pack of snow. She found it hard to find good footing as she grappled with her hands to keep from sliding. All of a sudden, the top layer that she was depending on gave way and began falling away, carrying Shirley with it. Down she tumbled, trying desperately to grab onto anything that would stop her descent. She knew that the cliff was below her and if she didn't stop, it would be her end. She clawed frantically with her finger nails.

She stood up dazed and disoriented. Her last memory was of floating in the state of motionlessness. Shirley looked around and wondered at the mound that stopped her from falling over the edge. She sat down, trying to get her bearings.

"What is this?" she whispered to herself. "It looks like a pile of stones that had been placed here intentionally."

She took a closer look and examined the stack from many angles.

"It's a cairn or memorial for someone who died," she said more out loud and with certainty. "Could this be for the boy that had fallen in her dream?" Shirley wondered.

Shirley was shaken to think that a shrine commemorating a dead person had saved her life. This acknowledgment though gave her a renewed desire to get to the top. Once again, she stood up, adjusted her pack and began to climb. She looked toward the pinnacle through the mist that blotted out the light.

"I think I'm pretty close. This time I'll make sure of every step I take."

The nearer she got to the summit, the daylight became brighter.

"I hope it's clear at the top."

The haze opened, revealing a bright craggy ledge where she could stand and look out at the vista. With the waning of the sun's radiance, the rocks and crevasses about her stood out with a brilliance. The girl clamored up the last few yards and stood on the shelf. The sun being at her back, she watched her shadow stretch out in front of her. To her surprise though, she noticed that there were two shadows instead of just one. She turned and saw Tyke standing next to her. It was a moment of sheer joy and elation.

As the sun was setting closer to the horizon, the shadow of the girl and deer stretched out over the mountain peaks finally merging into one. At the end of their shadow, could be seen a silhouette of a boy shaped in the clouds. She looked around, realizing the deer was nowhere in sight as if he had never been with her. She was alone now and her thoughts turned towards her home and family, who were far away across the mountains. What were they doing now? Were they missing her?

Shirley took out her GPS and texted, "I have arrived and I am safe. See you in a few days. Love, Shirley."

After standing for what seemed to be hours in the fading dusk, she finally understood the meaning of the painted box and her dream. She also became aware of the part that she had just played in helping the boy's spirit travel into the land beyond.

Darkness was settling in and it would be too dangerous for her to head back down, so Shirley decided to camp on the top that night. It would also mean she could stay close to the boy that she had dreamed about, who was now safely at the end of his Vision Quest. She couldn't fight the tears, realizing that this young man she had known so briefly would remain with her for the rest of her life and that this joining together would help her to complete her own Vision Quest.

CPSIA information can be obtained
at www.ICGtesting.com
Printed in the USA
LVOW04*0318091215
464650LV00001B/1/P